GARL

P9-CDS-963

Juniper Hill
School Library

The Story of
The Milky Way
~ A CHEROKEE TALE ~

by *Joseph Bruchac* and *Gayle Ross*
paintings by *Virginia A. Stroud*

DIAL BOOKS FOR YOUNG READERS NEW YORK

For all the children who have learned they must look before they can see   J.B.

To the memory of Grandmother Anne   G.R.

For Tana and Tsali, from Mom   V.A.S.

Published by Dial Books for Young Readers, A Division of Penguin Books USA Inc.
375 Hudson Street, New York, New York 10014
Text copyright © 1995 by Joseph Bruchac and Gayle Ross. Paintings copyright © 1995 by Virginia A. Stroud.
All rights reserved. Designed by Heather Wood.
Printed in Hong Kong
First Edition 1 3 5 7 9 10 8 6 4 2

Library of Congress Cataloging in Publication Data
Bruchac, Joseph, 1942–
The story of the Milky Way : a Cherokee tale / by Joseph Bruchac and Gayle Ross
paintings by Virginia A. Stroud. — 1st ed.
p.   cm.
ISBN 0-8037-1737-7. — ISBN 0-8037-1738-5 (lib. bdg.)
1. Cherokee Indians—Folklore. 2. Milky Way—Folklore. I. Ross, Gayle. II. Stroud, Virginia A. III. Title.
E99.C5B887   1995   398.2′089′975—dc20   94-20926   CIP   AC

The artwork was prepared with acrylic paint on Museum Rag paper.
It was then color-separated and reproduced in full color.

Illustrator's Note

THE ARTWORK FOR THIS BOOK depicts a period of history, the early 1800's, when the Cherokee people still lived in their homeland in the Smoky Mountains of Tennessee and Georgia. They had incorporated some parts of non-Indian culture—for instance, in this time the great Sequoya introduced the system that gave the Cherokee people their written language, and they had adapted their clothing from buckskin skirts and breech-cloths to the style of dress shown in my art—while retaining many traditional ways. While growing up in northeastern Oklahoma near the Cherokee capital of Tahlequah, I often saw examples of the clothing of this era; I own a turkey-feather cape given to me by the Keetoowah Society, similar to that worn by Beloved Woman in *The Story of the Milky Way.*

This historical period was short-lived; it ended with the forced removal of the Cherokee from their homeland in the late 1830's, the "Trail of Tears." In the belief that creation tales speak to all times, I have set *The Story of the Milky Way* in this time which interests me both as an artist and as a member of the Cherokee Nation of Oklahoma.

—VIRGINIA A. STROUD

The Origin of the Story

NUMEROUS CHEROKEE FRIENDS have shared this story with me over the years, including Robert Conley, a Cherokee novelist, and Jean Starr, a Cherokee poet, both of whom have included versions of the tale in their writing. Other versions of the story can be found in many published collections. One of the earliest is James Mooney's *Myths of the Cherokee* (1900).   — JOSEPH BRUCHAC

I FIRST LEARNED THIS STORY when I was a child, to share with my friends on a weekend camp-out. It appeared in a little booklet that had belonged to my grandmother, Anne Ross Piburn—which, I later learned, had been reprinted from the James Mooney collection. I also had a typed transcript of the story as Grandmother Anne, a Cherokee storyteller, had told it. In her version the emphasis was on the old couple and the anger felt by the people for anyone who would steal from the elderly. That is the way I have always told the story.

Joe Bruchac and I felt it was important to identify the elder who provides the solution to the riddle of the theft; the Beloved Woman would be the most honored of the elders among the Cherokee. We felt that not enough is known about the powerful women figures who are part of Cherokee tradition. We added the character of the grandson to our version to represent the love children everywhere feel for their grandparents.   — GAYLE ROSS

This is what the old people told me when I was a child.

LONG AGO when the world was new, there were not many stars in the sky.

In those days the people depended on corn for their food.

They would grind it and keep it in bins behind their homes. Bread made from the cornmeal often kept them from starving during the long winter months.

One morning an old man and an old woman went to their bin for some cornmeal. What they found there upset them very much. The lid was off the bin, the level inside had dropped by a handspan, and there was cornmeal scattered over the ground. Surely no one in the village would steal from the elders! Who could the thief be?

Now, the old couple had a young grandson who loved them very much. When he heard about the stolen cornmeal, he decided he would be the one to catch the thief.

That evening when Grandmother Sun had gone to her rest
and Elder Brother Moon was not yet in the sky, the boy went

to his grandparents' home. He hid near the bin of cornmeal and waited.

Late that night the boy saw an eerie light coming across the fields. When it was closer, he saw it was in the shape of a great dog. The dog nosed the lid off the bin and began to eat. When it had eaten its fill of the cornmeal, the dog turned and ran through the woods into the night.

The boy lay in his hiding place, not quite believing what his eyes had seen.

But in the morning, in the cornmeal scattered around the bin, he saw the tracks of a giant dog.

When the boy told the people what he had seen, no one knew what to do. So they decided to go to the Beloved Woman, a leader among the people. She was old and wise and understood many things.

When the Beloved Woman looked at the tracks, she said,
"These are the tracks of a creature like no dog on this earth. It is
a spirit dog and may have great power. We must be very careful."
The Beloved Woman instructed the people to gather all their
drums and turtleshell rattles.

"We will hide near the cornmeal bin and wait," she said. "When the giant dog comes, we will make a great noise. That will frighten it so badly, it will never return."

The people hurried to get their drums and rattles.

Then they hid near the old couple's cornmeal bin. It grew
dark and the few stars sparkled in the sky. Soon they saw

the shining form of the great spirit dog coming across the fields.

It was so big that many of the people were frightened and wanted to run, but the wise old woman whispered, "Do not be afraid. Only wait for my signal."

The great dog came to the bin and began to eat, filling its
big mouth with the white cornmeal.

"NOW!" the Beloved Woman shouted.

Then all the people rose up, beating their drums and shaking their rattles:

THUM-THUM THUM-THUM

SHISSH SHISSH SHISSH SHISSH

The noise was as loud as the Thunderer when he speaks. The great dog leaped in fear and began to run, but the people chased it, still beating their drums and shaking their rattles.

On and on the great dog ran, white cornmeal spilling from
its mouth.

It ran till it came to the top of a hill and then it leaped...up into the sky!

It ran across the sky until the people could see it no longer.
But the cornmeal that had spilled from its mouth remained

behind as a great band of light across the night sky.
Each grain of cornmeal that fell became a star.

Just as the Beloved Woman had said, the great dog never
returned to bother the people. But where it ran across the sky
was left that pattern of stars the Cherokee call *Gil'liutsun
stanun'yi* (Gil-LEE-oot-soon stan-UNH-yee), "the place where
the dog ran." That is how the Milky Way came to be.